BECOMING
A
CAPSTONE

THE
CORNERSTONE
PUBLISHING

OMOTOYOSI ADEBAYO

BECOMING A CAPSTONE

Cornerstone Publishing

A Division of Cornerstone Creativity Group LLC
Phone: +1(516) 547-4999
info@thecornerstonepublishers.com
www.thecornerstonepublishers.com

To order bulk of this book or to contact the author for speaking engagement please email:

omotoyosis@gmail.com

ACKNOWLEDGMENTS

Flying 30,000 feet above ground heading back home from my trip to New Jersey, thinking of all the people that have played significant roles in my life. I want to take this opportunity to acknowledge you all for your immense contributions, support and encouragement.

Thank you for helping me make this dream a reality. A special shoutout to my wife and daughter, my family, friends, colleagues, spiritual parents, uncles and aunties who have in no small measure, aided in the process of putting this book together. I also want to thank my publisher and publishing company for a job well done. I am forever indebted to you and I'm looking forward to the great things we will do next.

I love you all and I appreciate you.

Yours Truly,
Omotoyosi Adebayo

FOREWORD

The journey of life is full of twists and turns, ups and downs. As go you through this journey, you have to make several choices – career path, profession, marriage partner, where to live and, sometimes, the very difficult choice of having to venture into a very different terrain like traveling to a foreign country for "greener pastures".

The opportunity of leaving a "third world" country for a country like the USA seems an easy choice without fully understanding the culture shock and struggles that lie ahead. Nothing in life really prepares you for this unless of course you're very young. But for a grown adult family man, as told in this book, that is a very difficult move.

The author has done a masterful job of presenting this story to the readers in a fun and exciting way that helps the readers to learn a lot of life lessons. Chief of this is that there is no mountain too high nor valley to deep that you cannot conquer with determination and good sense.

One valuable takeaway for me is this. "Though your beginnings may be small, your latter end shall be greatly increased" (Job 8:7). You can make it in life, if you don't give up. This is the beautiful story captured in the book you have in your hands and hopefully you will read it.

I have been fortunate over the past few years to experience and share in the story the author portrays in this book. It is one of grits and raw determination that proves that, with God, we all can rise above our limitations and struggles in life.

God bless you and happy reading.

—Pastor Koye Sanni
RCCG Salvation Center, San Antonio

CONTENTS

PROLOGUE

A man's journey through life, especially in his quest for meaning and success, is both an adventure and a rollercoaster of highs and lows. The highs being those thrilling moments of achievement and excitement, while the lows are moments of miscalculations and misadventures. Either way, a man eventually grows through this "process" and turns out enviably right or despicably wrong. The choice, though, is exclusively his.

You are about to take a voyage into the psyche of an immigrant in search of greener pastures and very desperate about it. His transition from "innocence" to experience is deeply intriguing. It reveals life as a school from which we all learn lessons, one of which is to turn our pitfalls into speed bumps that prevent fatal collisions, while leading us on to our growth and eventual triumph.

This narrative demystifies failure and highlights the rewards of persistent effort - effort to be better and aspire higher, even in the face of serial letdowns. Above all, it redirects attention to the Ultimate Guide of destiny, who gives clarity to the unresolved issues of our lives and, most assuredly, gives wings and potency to our dreams.

One
BABY STEPS

It is often said that life is a journey; a trudge into a jungle full of not only people that are dreamers in their rights, but also of possibilities that have been bequeathed to humanity by the creator. This is to say that man was never thrust into the world to navigate this journey on his own. While he may, through his freewill, travel on his terms using his instinctive compass, enroute the seas, roads, rails and airways to both his destiny and destinations, the creator at different points, throws in a puzzle or two. He does so to remind him of his own humanity, and the need to stay connected to his life source. Besides the divinity of a journey is also the humanity and psychology of it. For man, a journey is first embarked upon in the mind, before it comes to physical manifestation.

This is the story of Segun, but before Segun was his father, Wole, whose desperate desire to escape the life he feared for the one he dreamt of, led him to the life he now lives and the life that his children have inherited, all because of one fateful and faithful journey.

Prior to Wole's hallowed journey to the United States in search of his own peculiar share of the American Dream, he had weighed his options as a civil servant in Nigeria with five kids and a wife to feed and cater for. And when he added himself to the sum, it would equal seven mouths to not only feed, but also to protect and guide. He had often imagined within himself how on earth people survived in such a country with so much uncertainty hanging in the air. How could he possibly smile and wave *"e k'aro" and "e ku'jo meta"* to the men and women who daily trudged to the mini market in front of his rented three-bedroom apartment in Lagos mainland? Men and women who in spite of their quaking sinews, dark-circled eyes that had seen better days, wounded pride and fragile hopes, met and greeted him cheerfully on his way to catch the early morning bus to Victoria Island.

"Ah, my *broda*, how was your night?" cooed Baba Mutiu, the man that ran the small bakery opposite the house. "I *dey jare. I just wan* run to the junction and join the staff bus or take a taxi if I have missed it," replied Wole. The amazing thing about this early morning greetings and banters was that they said the exact same things every day, nothing new and nothing spontaneous. Sometimes it was exchanged as a matter of courtesy - flat, no emotions and hurriedly done; other days they were intense, genuine and cheerfully exchanged. But lately, everyone merely observed courtesy just to keep from doing any other thing that might jeopardize their relationships. The frustration was so thick that if not cushioned with pleasantries, people might helplessly transfer their aggressions on one another.

Wole went to work every day and came home with the deep-seated fear of what turn life would take after retirement. He wondered how he would take care of his wife and five children and other lives that benefited from his success. He would daily go to the office to face the uninspiring faces of co-workers who only made his fears to come alive and even grow wings. They would chat endlessly about ex-colleagues who either came down with a stroke or went bankrupt servicing one medical bill or the other. His own retirement loomed around the corner and he had nothing to fall back on. With a salary like his, which was never enough to cover family expenses, how could he possibly save or even have enough to invest in anything? His last child, Segun, a budding superstar, daily shared his dreams about a glorious future with him. But all he could do was gaze into his dreamy eyes and shiver at the thought of the possibility of Segun's dreams drying up like the morning dew even before the sun kissed it.

The economic situation of Nigeria choked every plan he had come up with to cushion the fear that congested his confused mind daily as an imminent retiree. Every passing day, he shuddered at the possibility of losing his capacity to provide for his household. He drew up plans alone in the middle of the night, scribbling for hours unending, and then tore them up as soon as they were completed, nothing worked, and the signs of the time were not in his favor. Segun would lie on his stomach, eyes dimmed as he stares at his father, wondering why he couldn't write without tearing up so many sheets of paper. His siblings would deliberately check out the dustbin in the morning, all to find it empty, no thanks to their proactive mother. Mosun would wake to a trash full of crumpled paper, and her beloved husband lying next to the heap on the floor and she would quickly perform her quick sanitation routine of clearing the heap. She had come to love this man who constantly penned his thoughts, plans and every other thing in between.

****

Segun dressed for school in a lack-luster manner. From the way things fell from his hands, it was obvious to everyone that either he didn't want to go to school on that very day, or something or someone weighed heavily on his mind. The rest of the family dug into their oatmeal and bean-cake breakfast as

16

plates and spoons engaged in friendly dialogs, clanging away while Segun sulked in the corner, caressing his oatmeal with his spoon while nibbling on his bean-cake without lifting sizable portions of the items to his mouth. Kemi, Taiwo, Kehinde and Tayo emptied their bowls and dashed off to school as their *"byebye"* trailed off, leaving behind, Segun, whose school was a stone throw from the house.

Mosun rushed out of the room, all dressed up and ready to head out. Wole followed behind her, rubbing his stomach and ready to devour his breakfast. But they both stopped in their tracks to examine Segun who was lost in thoughts, hand held unto the spoon with which he stirred his food in a directionless motion.

"Segun what is the matter?" Wole inquired, as Mosun's worried voice followed suit.

"Segun, are you alright?" she said, resting her hand on his forehead and neck repeatedly, in a bid to ascertain his bodily temperature, in order to rule out fever. After a long pause, and restless turning of shoulders just so he could gently wriggle free from his mother's hands, Segun finally said, "They left me behind."

"Who are the "they" that left you behind?" Wole asked, trying hard to mask his impatience. Mosun calmly listened on, urging him on with her facial expressions.

"Daniel and Mabel have relocated with their parents to

Canada. They were my close friends. Now I have no friends in school" he said, looking away, head bowed as he continued talking.

"They told me after our Common Entrance Examination. We planned to attend the same secondary school, but they have left me behind", lamented Segun, visibly ruffled at the admission of his own loneliness and aloneness.

"They have not left you behind; they only relocated Segun. Move on dear, I promise you will meet them someday," Wole encouraged his son, though a bit lost in thoughts himself. He fixed his own breakfast and ate with Segun, all the while staring into space. Both men walked to school that morning, in silence, deriving strength and courage from the comfort of their hugged palms and interlocked fingers. Both men parted ways at the school gate, waving goodbye with a poor attempt at smiling, Segun pensive and Wole, lost thoughts. No words were exchanged all through the long walk, but Segun appreciated the silent company that his father offered often hen his spirit was in dire need of a boost.

****

While it seemed as Segun's little episode at the breakfast table had ended, as abruptly as it had begun, that incident gave Wole a new insight and angle for

18

possible consideration. One fateful day, he stretched and yawned loudly and dramatically as Mosun rushed from the kitchen to the bedroom to find out if he was alright.

"Wole, are you okay?"

He ignored her completely while laughing hysterically. She moved to the corner where the trash can was and there were no crumpled sheets of paper. She placed her hand on his neck to check for his temperature, but he was normal and laughed louder at her reaction.

"Mosun, can't a man just wake up feeling good? Why are you being dramatic?"

"Hmmm, this is unlike you. There are no crumpled papers, what did you stay awake doing all night, Wole?" Mosun asked, still staring at her happy husband in confusion.

"I stayed up, thinking about my life and future without putting pen to paper. I was right here in my head all night" he said, repeatedly hitting the left side of his head with his ring finger.

"So what changed between last night and this morning that has brought so much excitement to your face?" Mosun inquired, gradually catching on with the excitement.

"Remember fifteen years ago when everyone kept disturbing me to find a way and leave the country so I can make enough to keep things running back home?"

"Yes, I remember, go on…" replied impatient Mosun.

"Well. I am finally tired of the country and ready to make that big and dreaded move" he said, his smile gradually thinning out.

"I will believe you when I see you consistently making the effort to leave, without giving up. I will not have you get my hopes high and dash them again. I remember trying hard to convince you years back to make this move but you agreed and backed out without taking the first step," she said walking back to the kitchen.

"Mosun, I don't need you to believe me or prompt me to do this, I am fed up and the only thought that rekindled my hope is the thought of leaving this country for good".

"What will happen to the kids and me? Where are we in the scheme of things or are you going to leave us here?" she asked a trifle impatiently.

"No, my love, we are all leaving but at different times. I will go first and work for a while during which I will lay the foundation for you and the kids to come over".

"How exactly do you plan to do this, or do you have

any plans that you are not willing to share?" asked Mosun, staring at him suspiciously.

"I had a long call last night. I spoke with Badmus, my best friend from years back, he now pastors a revival church in Dallas and has promised to send me an invitation with which to apply for visa, dear. I love you too much to marry another woman. Besides my Christian faith does not permit such deception. So, relax and let me figure out how and when to start the process" Wole said, staring her in the eyes.

She smiled a little, without showing to what extent his words gladdened her heart. "God will definitely see this plan of yours to a successful execution. Please how do I come in and what do you need me to help with?"

"In every way you can imagine, I need your support and prayers, my love".

Mosun nodded and more out of seeing her husband's frustration gradually lifting than for the idea of him travelling out of the country. Something had got to be going well for Wole, and if travelling out of the country was that thing, then so be it. Mosun's mind weighed the idea of having Wole, who had never spent a night without her all of their marital lives, and had never been a fan of travel, nor had he ever embarked on one without her, now toying with the idea of travelling as far as the United States to spend some years apart from her.

She thought of all the things that could go wrong with this promising move. She thought of failure; what if Wole never made enough to sponsor the entire family to join him? What if he met and fell for another woman, possibly a white woman? Even with their devoted membership to the Intercessory unit of their church, Mosun's fears on the possibility of her husband straying from the path of the faith in his relationship with women, was rooted in family history. Wole's father had married many wives and though Wole suffered the consequences of such a family setup, and never hesitated to tell Mosun just how much he detested polygamy, Mosun could not but fear what loneliness in a cold country could do to men of faith. She remembered his assurance and shrugged off all the negativity clouding her mind, and started thinking about all the things that could go right. They were a strong and devoted Christian home and nothing of such would ever happen. Wole's plans would work out for the good of the entire family.

All the while, Segun stood by the corner, staring from Mosun to Wole, trying hard to wrap his little head around this 'next level' and how it would affect their lives. He was the last born, his father's right-hand man and his mother's hand bag. He wondered where he stood in the whole plan.

Just then, Mosun dashed into their bedroom, picked up her pen and paper and began drafting a rough estimate of the cost of this decision. This move would take more than half of their savings, but it was worth the sacrifice. Mosun braced herself for the challenges ahead. She would be the mother, mentor, father and guardian of five children while performing her professional duties as an accountant in a multi-national company. She shuddered at the thought of the overwhelming responsibilities ahead and the thought of going through months, and most likely years without Wole in close proximity. For the next one month, she would add, subtract, multiply and divide from this very paper painstakingly making sure that Wole's expenditures are appropriately managed so that the family doesn't slip into financial crisis, especially with resumption and school fees season looming close.

Wole walked into the room all dressed and ready to travel down to Federal Government College, Kwale, north of Nigeria, where his son had sat for oral and written interviews. He was so excited at the prospect of his last child entering secondary school. He couldn't contain his excitement and had been beaming with smiles. Wole's father could barely feed his teeming battalions adequately, let alone give them proper education, a home in which his mother took turns with other women to get her husband's attention even during the times she had to discuss school-related issues. Once Baba's children managed to complete high school, they were thrown into the jungle of life, unprepared, unaccompanied and ill-equipped to navigate life on their own.

Wole was fortunate enough to attend the School of Forestry and gained the very certification that earned him a job in the agricultural sector. Now ready to travel to the United States to begin a new life that would pave the way for the entire family to join him, he could not help but to ensure that the academic needs of his children were met, as well as seeing that every other aspect of his family life was in order before his much-awaited journey. He pulled his son Segun closer, tucked in his shirts properly, knotted his ties and laced up his shoes.

Segun was a very smart kid and Wole had sworn to make sure that Segun channeled his intelligence effectively and become great in future. Wole loved and advocated for education. He bore the burden of the uneducated people in his life - the constant calls to send money for this and that, so much that he had a monthly allowance set aside for extended family demands. Seeing where he came from and how far he had come due to the little education he acquired, he vowed that all his children would go to school. Mosun stared at father and son briefly in admiration before getting lost in thoughts again.

"Segun, you have grown into an intelligent and strong boy. I am so proud of you son" Wole said, overcome with joy and admiration.

"Thank you, Daddy," said Segun, feeling awkward at how his disciplinarian father was suddenly going all emotional on him and his siblings lately. He figured that it must be the travel and the fact that his visa application came through. From what the coordinator of the entrance examination said, Segun had answered his questions brilliantly and was sure to be given admission to one of the best unity schools in Nigeria.

Wole and his family chatted boisterously as they drove to the post office to check the list of students on merit list. Segun, who was in high spirits, properly dressed with the plan of dropping by a studio to take his passport photograph, and drop by the Ekiti State liaison office in Lagos to pick his evidence of state of origin, was the happiest of the crew. Wole felt a certain kind of relief at the prospect of his last child gaining admission and resuming ahead of his travel. His satisfaction at how he had succeeded in putting all outstanding parental responsibilities in order, brought so much fulfillment.

25

On getting to the post office, Wole checked the entire admission list but his son's name, Segun Bankole, was not there. He checked the section for candidates selected based on catchment area, his name was not there. He went further to the section for students selected from "educationally disadvantaged states of north-north and south-south Nigeria" - never mind that he is from the south-west - his name was absent. He stared at his son's face, at the frustration gradually building up on his face and composed himself.

"Segun, there must be a mistake somewhere or maybe there will be second list. Go and sit with your mother in the car, I will handle this. Wole called the woman that he had chosen to be his son's guardian upon resumption. She picked at the first ring.

"Mrs. Ojo, Segun's name is not on the list oo" he spat, visibly trying to control his temper.

"Did you check well, Sir? Check again and let me know the outcome" she replied

"*Haba*, Madam! I am not a child *na*, I said his name is not there. I have checked over and over. *Ejoor* what do I do? Will they release another list?" he flipped, allowing his anger to gain the upper hand.

"I am sorry but that is the only list. And it is a combination of the lists from the slots given to the

26

president, government and some top stakeholders in government parastatals. So no more lists. Did you meet or settle anyone to secure your son's place?" Mrs. Ojo quizzed, with a tinge of irritation in her voice.

"Besides the fact that it is against my principles, Segun is the best student in his class and has never failed any form of written or oral examination or interview. So why should I bribe for admission?"

"I take it that this is your first encounter with this kind of arrangement. So, I will be open to avoid a future occurrence. There are some wealthy men whose children can never pass this exam, so they pay for other people's result and admission to be sold to them. While your son may be a genius, if you do not pay to secure his admission and result, you will be shocked that his intelligence is not enough. I wish we had this discussion earlier, Sir". She said with a tone of finality that signaled the end of discussion to Wole.

Wole ended the call, his frustration evident in his quick strides to the direction of the car. He paced up and down, thinking of a perfect way of passing the message across to the already ruffled Segun. He entered the car, started the engine and headed in the direction of home. They drove in silence for a few seconds and he suddenly said, "You know what, I have changed my mind about that school, I will be far away from home and you all in a month's time. As much as possible, I want my family to be close. It will be only your mum closely taking care of you all very soon; as much as possible, I don't want her to worry so much about you. Segun, you will attend one of the best schools in Lagos where mummy can easily enter the car and visit you should there be any need for emergency visits". They all caught his drift and drove in silence till they got home.

****

The silence in the home of the Bankoles increased by the day. It was obvious to Wole, the vacuum that his absence would create, and he was trying to assure everyone that his telephone conversations would be consistent and enough to cushion the distance from Nigeria to America.

Segun was expectedly the most affected. He had always been close to his father, being the last child of the family. And his siblings would sometimes use him to get favors from their parents. And while Mosun and Wole may be disciplinarians who will not always spare the rod and spoil their children, they however loved their children so much and will make great sacrifices to keep them happy. The decision to travel to the United States was birthed by the urgent need to give his children the best.

The packed bags at one corner of the room, Mosun's constant inquisitions as she tried to find out if Wole had packed one item or the other, didn't help the anxious mood looming around the house. The children embraced the coming changes with mixed feelings; while the prospect of relocation came with its peculiar thrills, the thrills were soon watered down by the unsavory rhythms of absence and distance. But as the days drew near, everyone came to terms with this promising change and embraced the possibilities that came with it. There were moments of tears and doubts; uncertainty hung in the air, hovering around the home of the Bankoles like a thick cloud heavily pregnant with tomorrow's rain. But once the mini-van loaded with all of Wole's personal effects and belongings hit the road enroute the Murtala Mohammed International Airport, there was no looking back.

With a hand luggage full of foiled fried chicken, two bottles of water, a magazine and a giant-sized King James Version of the Bible, and two roller boxes, the transparent glass partition that separated the travelers from accompanying by-standers, was the only obstacle that stood between Wole, his wife and his five children. Mosun and the children waved endlessly and cried while Wole sorted himself out in the departure area of the Murtala Mohammed International Airport. They had arrived the airport at 8:30pm for an 11pm flight.

Segun was the quietest of the crew. He merely stared ahead in silence, visibly unhappy but unable to surrender to, the pool of tears threatening to flow down from his eyes. He merely stared on, blinking back repeatedly. As Wole waved his hands and finally marched out of sight, the Bankoles drove home, and their journey back home was as silent as their journey to the airport.

Two
THE FORERUNNER

Now in his one-bedroom apartment, all Wole could think of was survival. He had retired at 40, and had invested all his life's savings into this epic journey. He had promised his wife the night before his travel that he would work hard, save up and start the process that would bring the rest of the family over to the states and also get a bigger apartment while at it. But America had dealt him an unexpected blow and beyond his hallowed expectations and plans, were the obstacles of age and certification.

Wole neither schooled in America nor did he acquire the best of education while in Nigeria. So, he considered himself lucky when the church within his neighborhood kindly offered him an administrative position. He worked diligently and tirelessly to the admiration of co-workers. He spoke with his family almost every day. He advised, instructed, prayed and cajoled them at different points. On almost every occasion, however, he noticed that Segun sounded withdrawn. He was neither happy nor angry to hear from him, unlike his siblings who were thrilled at the stories shared by their father and even more satisfied at the fact that he was keeping to his promise of regularly checking on his family through calls.

One day, unable to keep his observation to himself any longer, Wole asked, "Segun, what is troubling you? Are you not happy to hear from me?"

"Daddy, you have said good things about America. You have not told us the bad stories," Segun replied.

"That is because there are no bad stories to share," Wole said, hoping he sounded convincing enough.

"Really, Daddy?" Segun pressed further. Or you want to save us the bad stories? Well, as for me, I am doing well in my new school and my teacher has taken an interest in me. I also have the challenge of making new friends. Daddy, you tell us only good things about America and not a single sad event. Daddy, is America so different from Nigeria that it has no troubles at all?"

Wole kept mute for a very long time and Segun continued.

"Daddy I am more worried about the things you are not telling us; that is why I am this calm."

"Then celebrate my good times and commit the ones you did not hear in God's hands. None of us can change certain things but God can" Wole finally managed to say.

"I always pray for you, Daddy and I will never stop," Segun said.

"Then that is enough for me. With your prayers, there is no mountain that God cannot move" Wole replied.

"May God protect you, Daddy," Segun prayed.

"And may he make way for me to take a walk with you down the streets of Dallas on days when the house cannot contain your emotions" Wole said and chuckled a little.

Segun suddenly giggled at the thought of the house not containing his emotions. He remembered the strolls across the streets of Ogba with his father. He giggled some more and that warmed Wole's heart. His last child was too old for his age and a bundle of emotions. He missed not being able to take him for a walk on days when he came down with one complaint or the other. It was almost like the boy often blackmailed him into taking such walks by coming up with one reason or the other to be alone on the street with him, away from the chatter and banter of his elder siblings.

He hung up the phone, feeling more fulfilled than ever

and more resolved to conquer whatever life in America threw at him. Segun had that effect on him. And Segun unintentionally planted the idea of immigration in his mind. He yearned even more to be with his family but had to shrug it off and get back to his routine.

****

The city of Dallas welcomed Wole, and amidst its fascinating splendor which marveled and its fast-paced metropolitan life, which was less herculean than Lagos, lay a certain unfamiliarity that unsettled him. He buried himself in his administrative roles and found solace in the many times he picked up his phone to engage in his extensive telephone conversations with his beloved wife and children.

Those long calls made him more resolute in his pursuit of familial dreams and happiness. The nostalgia after the goodbyes, the many memories that flooded his mind like caged birds let loose on a beautiful spring morning and the clarity and focus that beyond leaving the country, came with living for something, consoled his soul. He would pick up his Bible and revisit divine promises he had read with his family during their past family devotions. Rereading them came with new insights and angles of meaning every single time. The sheer ecstasy of unearthing something new, felt like discovering diamonds from a repeatedly dug land.

This was a sign that his new land of labor would yield good harvest.

Most importantly, he had begun to open up to Segun, on some of his struggles because he would always ask him for a balance of his reality in America. And unlike the rest of his siblings, he wasn't particularly thrilled by the thrills of the new life. No matter how Wole seasoned the narratives, Segun would probe further and Wole would yield, trusting him not to spill.

****

It was an unusually cold morning, with signs of the first chink of winter. Wole had dreaded and fantasized all at once about winter. He had bought his protective clothing and had been waiting eagerly and now he observed the first signs of snow. He parted the curtains and observed the tiny flakes that quickly melted upon falling on his window panes. He smiled and picked up his phone. He dialed Mosun's line and after the second ring, her sweet voice serenaded his ear.

"Wole" she said and paused.

"Hello dear, you won't believe it but I just witnessed my first snowfall."

"Really?"

"Yea! Though it is not in full swing, it still feels good

to witness something new. I have a feeling that I will love this weather, Mo," he said beaming with smiles.

"You see, I told you that you would adapt. Your children are sleeping. Wole junior has been very great with the fatherly role; he coordinates his siblings well, though he is still stubborn. Kehinde and Taiwo are doing great in school. Nike made her first soup and stew yesterday!" she said giggling excitedly

"This is great news but aren't you forgetting somebody?" he quizzed further, not hiding his curiosity.

"Oh, that one, he is still a big baby, he stayed up when I hinted that I would be speaking with you. He misses you so much and he's still a little morose, often refusing to do alone the things that you two did together. I have tried every method possible to pacify him but he remains unmoved. He is here waiting to speak with you. Let me give him the phone dear" she said, handing the phone to Segun.

"Daddy, good evening from Nigeria!" he said, his lips growing into a smile. Mosun spotted the sudden change of mood and snapped her fingers in his face, causing him to broaden the smile.

"Segun, why is the greeting coming from Nigeria and not you?" he said, dramatically feigning ignorance.

"Daddy, the time zones are different, so I am greeting

you in Nigerian time. Good evening from Nigeria, Daddy. Is it time for snowfalls already? Remember, you promised me a picture."

"Good morning from America, Segun. Once everywhere is covered in snow, I will snap and send to you but on one condition" he said, sounding a little serious.

"What is it, Daddy?"

"Promise me you will go about your classes, homework and house chores, cheerful and happy, like you did while I was at home. Your mother is worried about the change in your mood since I travelled, and it is affecting her. Do we have a deal?"

"Deal" he muttered, exchanging a quick glance with his mum, while fluttering his eyelids.

"Then get ready to receive more than snowfall pictures from me" he said.

Segun screamed and dashed off, handing his mother the phone.

"Ife, why do I feel like there is more that you want to tell me but holding back because of the distance between us? See, there is a lot I can do from over here, I want to be part of the joys and pains; I want to commend our children's excellence and condemn their misbehavior. I may be a distant father, but I don't want to be an absent father. How are you coping with your accounting job and the children? I know we planned and put a lot of things in place but I need toe know when any of our plans fail. Be open with me and tell me how you feel at every point, emotionally and otherwise. I want to be involved hundred percent. And see…"

"Wole, you worry too much. I said everything is fine; you have got to trust me to handle things from this end. Just focus on working to ensure the entire family is united again. Stop worrying your small round head" she teased, laughing out loud.

"The head is no longer small oo, with the *kain waka waka and plans wey this head carry ehn, e don big*" he said, laughing at his poor attempt at Pidgin English.

"It is well, my Love, God will do it for us and perfect all that concerns us, in Jesus' name, amen!" she cooed.

"Amen! I gotta run to work. Have a lot of paper works to handle. That reminds me, I got a second job though. But please don't ask me what it is" he said, sounding audibly in haste.

"Look who is advocating for openness? *Abeg* tell me about it when next you call," she said.

"O d'abo, *Ife mi?*" he said and dashed off.

38

****

Days turned into months, months into a year and gradually, the tied and knotted bonds of passion and familial love, held fastened over years by presence and involvement became weakened by absence and distance. The calls reduced as the pressures of working two jobs and trying hard to manage and save enough began to take a toll on Wole.

Mosun was very understanding, as there were times she could have complained; times she felt so lonely and alone but she carried on gallantly, ever so lively over the phone, while masking her pains, struggles and challenges in hearty giggles that warmed Wole's weary heart and worked like painkillers in his frail sinews, rekindling his resolve to struggle on and work harder at making this dream materialize.

There is indeed nothing like a woman who understands the ways of the world and how it reduces a man to a shadow of himself. Mosun deliberately chose to be an energizer, a tonic that spurred her man unto greater level of focus, while she covered for him at the home front.

Segun, on his part, was unflinching in his resolve to stay connected with his father. He would stay awake and wait for his call even if it meant pretending to be reading while his siblings slept. He would keep his eyes glued to the tabletop phone, like kids wait for Santa at Christmas. He would pounce on the phone at the slightest buzz.

"Hello Daddy," he would say, breathless and confounded by his own excitement.

"Segun... are you still awake. I thought you would be sleeping by now," his father would manage.

"I achieved something while keeping vigil, Daddy. I have been reading all night" he would say in his defense.

"That is good to know. What of your mother?"

"She slept off while waiting for your call, Dad. She is right beside me on the couch"

"Then we must not wake her up. She needs the rest. I will call back early in the morning"

"No, Dad. These calls do a lot for Mum. I am certain that she wouldn't mind me waking her up just so she can hear from you. If it didn't mean much to her, she would have slept off in the room" Segun said while waking up his mum. Mosun would spring up from the cushion, nearly tripping on her clothes.

"Mum, Daddy is on the phone let me say goodbye and hand you the phone."

"Segun... You behave like an old man, ah! So you are now your mother's husband abi?" Wole would say.

"Okay, Dad. I am okay now and yes, I will now go to bed. Mum is awake and will now continue with you. Good evening, Dad," he would say.

"It is morning Segun. Good morning, my son, and be good okay?"

"Always, Dad, I will remain good" he would say, handing the phone over to his Mum.

"I see your deputy husband is doing a great job now dear" Wole teased Mosun, laughing heartily

"That one, don't mind him, he pretended to be sleeping until I slept off. And not just Segun, they have all been wonderful, and so supportive" Mosun said.

"I didn't expect you to say anything different. You have not reported anything negative since I left. While I am happy about it, I hope that is the true situation dear. So tell me about you sleeping on the couch. You must be so tired, dear" Wole observed.

"I won't lie to you, my whole body feels like a trailer drove over it. Even with how close my office is, I was sleeping and waking in traffic. I had to walk all the way home with my handbag and bag of groceries in hand. Thank God I didn't drive…" Mosun lamented.

"Get some rest sweetheart. I will call tomorrow. Have a restful night darling."

****

A year turned into years and the struggle became real. And as years turned into years, boys became young men and girls became ladies. Wole became to his children, another voice at the end of the line but nonetheless their father. Mosun on the other hand became a father, mentor, mother, the astute disciplinarian and a lover to her now adolescent children, counseling, guiding and guarding when needed. She felt the emotional vacuum created by Wole's physical absence, especially as the calls came in more out of obligation and responsibility.

They were physically and emotionally drained at both ends but kept hope alive. They often prayed, shed silent tears, and had long conversations in which the children took turns to talk to their father. But they recognized in broad terms, each member of the family, and the increasing strain on the very bonds that held them all together. But they were each willing to try and wait until breakthrough came, the much awaited miracle of reuniting with their father, Wole Bankole.

Three
TRIUMPHAL ENTRY

After years of waiting, Wole, who had earlier filed for his family to come over to the United States, finally received the news of a lifetime and called his wife Mosun to inform her.

"Hello, Dad. Good evening," Segun said.

"Evening, son. Do you sleep by the phone? You are always the first to pick up Segun" Wole asked, puzzled at the unyielding spirit of a son that had won his heart over and over with his love.

"Just making sure your calls don't go unanswered" he teased, giggling while handing the phone to his mother.

"Guess what, Mosun?" Wole said, not willing to spill the good news just immediately.

"The coast is finally clear for us to come join you, *abi?*" Mosun said, excitement flying like fireflies on a windy night.

"Yes, my dear!" Wole yelled. "Tell the kids and let's start our plans of renewing passports and shopping tomorrow. Please get some sleep. I have to head to work now. Good night, my darling."

"Good night, Love" Mosun uttered with palpable joy.

She held the phone to her chest, running her fingers along its spiral wires. Segun who was typically by the corner, moved closer and hugged her mum who surrendered completely to her son's embrace, as she circled her hands along his long trunk.

The children welcomed the news with mixed feelings as the endless waiting had already made them come to terms with the possibility of failure and they had gotten accustomed to having their father far away, while their mum ran the home. They began preparations here in Nigeria while Wole got a bigger apartment. He had earlier shown his children round the beautiful apartment in a video call and even assured them that the views from every corner of the house was more breathtaking and they would love it.

Gradually the children's excitement grew by the day as their friends told them how lucky they were to be traveling to such a country that held greater prospects for immigrants, and wished to be in their shoes. Mosun made sure she bought all that the family would be needing, from foodstuffs to clothing and other necessities that would make the transition from Nigerian to American ways less challenging. She sent most of their heavy carrier boxes and *Ghana-must-go* bags to the airport in order to cargo them ahead of their already dated trip.

On the eve of their departure, select family members and close-knit church members were invited to attend the sendoff ceremony, officiated by the regional pastor of their church outside their residence, just beside the mini wagon loaded for the short trip to the airport.

The Bankoles' trip to the airport was as silent as the initial trip in which they accompanied Wole to the airport. Tensions mounted over anxiety as members of this beautiful family silently occupied their minds with all the possibilities that awaited them in their new home. The children had a tough night the day before their journey, as they sat around the center table in the living room, creating scenarios and taking turns to say how they would react if caught under such circumstances. The American movies they had watched for years, provided material and background for their imaginations to run wild and resolve complex challenges. But little did they know that the world of make-belief, even in its crudest form, was far more attractive than reality and they were about to journey into a society which though prided itself in freedom is by far the most complex society. They would in time

45

realize that the Statue of Liberty with its outstretched hand of fire, symbolizing freedom, also had around its unshackled feet, the iron chain of limitation.

The Statue of Liberty connoted many possibilities. The real threshold between appearance and reality was multi layers of façade, and once the smokescreen cleared, reality dawned on man.

"I think I will finally get a handshake from Denzel Washington and maybe take a selfie with Oprah Winfrey or maybe Whoopi Goldberg," said Taiwo. "Those guys would finally breathe the same air with me. Oh my goodness, there is no way I would be anything but great, just like them."

"Me, I will just end up as a cute newscaster or reporter at BBC" said Kehinde.

"BBC is in the United Kingdoms, not the United States," Segun chipped in, as his elder ones continued laughing out loud in spite of the fears brewing inside them.

"Professor Segun! Whatever! Whether Kingdom or States, they are all United! If BBC is not there, I would join CNN or even work at the White House. I have to think bigger now" Taiwo retorted as they all burst out laughing, and Segun managed a good laugh this time, as Kehinde went on cracking the entire family up with how she would carry herself once in America.

"Thank God, I already eat iceblock here," Kehinde said. "So, I will be so unaffected by the cold. I will probably just eat snow, instead of having Mum chase me around for scooping ice from the freezer with a spoon. I will sneak out at night and take a handful of America's white glory!" Everyone burst out laughing again. They were so used to having the twins entertain them with their jokes.

"Snow is the white man's dust and the brown dust of the earth is ours," Taiwo chipped in. "How can you dream of eating dust, twinny?"

"Their earth is winter's deep freezer. I will just help clear the ground by shoveling off a handful, just a handful" Kehinde joked again, as another bout of laughter welcomed her statement.

"What a dream! From the BBC to CNN and now she wants to be a snow woman, shoveling snow into her mouth but with bare hands, not a shovel like in the movies. My sister is a genius!" Segun teased and they roared with laughter, more because the joke came from their ever introspective youngest brother, the loner himself.

Mosun couldn't help herself, she smiled at their jokes. She listened from the hallway to the kitchen where she sat on the floor, silently regarding her soon-to-be ex-home. She smiled and was sometimes left wide-eyed at some of her children's expressions.

It had been years of distance between her and Wole and as much as she was excited about this trip, the more the days drew near, the more her heart thudded almost violently in her chest. She had conducted the evening devotion, visibly appearing happy, almost like her joy would fly out of her chest. Years of being a one man soldier in single parenthood had taught Mosun to successfully bury and sometimes mask her deepest emotions of fear and cravings for companionship.

And now, imagining being close to her husband gave her goose bumps, she felt like a newborn approaching the breast, like a suckling learning how to suck again after a long separation from her source of food. But her joys far outweighed her fears and she looked up to the future with so much hope and positivity. The worst and lonely days were behind.

Segun snuckaway from the group of dreamers, jokers and spectators, to Mosun as he wrapped his hands around her in a warm hug, just what Mosun needed.

"Mummy, everything will be fine, you just watch" he assured, with the certainty of a navigator who had a strong record of discovering new places.

****

At the airport, they weighed their hand luggage and few boxes and all was within the acceptable limit on the scale; subsequently, they were allowed to board. It would be the children's first trip by air, but they appeared visibly unruffled by the prospects of this adventure. They were all focused on the very green light at the end of their years of waiting to reunite with their father and for greener pastures, so much that the fatigue and nausea usually experienced by first timers while airborne never surfaced.

Kehinde and Taiwo who were afraid of heights and hated enclosures slept through the entire journey. And so sound and peaceful was their sleep that they found it in their young minds to snore while at it. Mosun was completely absorbed in the book of Psalms. She prayed while periodically turning around to check on her children as they were not sitting in close seats. Segun busied his ears with cool lyrics sipping in through the earphones of his mother's phone, eyes shut and with no care in the world. For him, fortune had finally opened his doors to his family and from now on, they would never be separated nor would they lack anything as seven good adult heads were surely better than two. The flight was not without a little turbulence owing to the weather but the Bankoles hardly noticed.

****

When Wole finally met his family at the airport, he couldn't believe his eyes. They had all grown and his little Segun was now taller than he was. They hugged him tight, refusing to step out of his embrace. Mosun stood behind and watched, tears gathered into a pool in her eyes. Both father and children remained in that embrace for a long while before turning to meet Mosun who, for once, in a long while let down her guard, visibly vulnerable to her own now streaming tears and emotions.

Wole met her in a hug of reassurance. Her chest pounded and her stomach rumbled at his close touch. She noticed the trembling of his cold hands as they wrapped around her waist. The couple had aged considerably, sporting few grey hairs and creases here and there and Wole's skin, though smooth, shiny and even fairer had a touch of age about it. Mosun looked younger than he was, but her eyes seemed sunken with stress lines and dark circles.

They drove in silence to their new home. The children peered through the car window, propping out their heads from both sides to see and point at the fascinations of their new country. Wole fastened his grip around Mosun's hand as their fingers wrapped around each other as though locked tight in an embrace through their hands. He slowly drove to their new home, chest pounding through his skin in a rhythm of in and out, up and down, like pestle repeatedly hitting a mortar.

Segun sat in the middle, staring at everyone and weighing his father's words over the phone in which he told him that he would have to start college from scratch once he got to America in order to acquire a certification that would make him employable after college and give him an edge over those applying to work with foreign degrees. His siblings were all working in Nigeria and their father had told them they would all take professional exams after which they would start their job hunt and in time, and once employed and credit worthy, they would try getting their second and third degrees.

He stared at his mum in admiration of all she had been to all five of them, and their father, a pillar of support, a beacon of light shining in Nigeria and across the Atlantic, all the way to America. He respected her for her resolve to keep it all together and make her family not walk but fly. He turned his gaze to his father and felt an equal admiration for putting himself out as a sacrificial lamb, a forerunner who had gone ahead to prepare the way so that he and his siblings could make it to the land of dreams. And while he might have felt anger for how long it took his father to get them over, all he felt at the moment for him was love and admiration.

But Segun also felt pity for his mum and dad, wondering how awkward it must feel trying to rekindle doused embers and enliven feelings of love that had been scorched by the harsh sun of Nigeria and frozen by years of winter in America. It would be like unlocking a treasure chest long buried away beneath the sea or in the deep grounds of some jungle. But seeing their hands shakily and awkwardly entangled was both a sign and a promise that they would surely meet each other half and eventually all the way.

Segun sighed in relief and looked up to find his father staring at him through the mirror while waiting for the traffic light to take the stages from red to yellow and then shine green. Life would be forever green for the Bankoles, and would always show them green light, Segun hoped, before winking at his dad, who winked back, as Mosun smiled while catching a glimpse of the brief exchange.

Wole turned after the intersection, and drove into the boulevard flanked by houses on both sides and announced to the children that they were finally home. For Segun, this indeed was a triumphal entry into the land of dreams and possibilities and he resolved to shine in this land. And contrary to his inner argument earlier on, on whether to address this new land as home, as soon as the car grinded to a halt, he looked around and announced, "We are home!"

Four
PRODIGAL PROFILING

Within months, Wole's elder children got placements that flung them across the cities of the United States, where they stayed with relatives and family friends, while taking up their new roles. They evaluated their certificates and began the process of higher degrees of Masters and PhD while at their respective jobs.

Segun naturally became the center of attention at home. And to everyone's surprise, he had moved from being a seeming introvert to a complete extrovert. Sensing trouble, his father quickly started the process of confining him to home and life rules. Wole had sworn to protect his children from anything that could kill their dreams, endanger their lives and future, or tarnish the family name that generations of ancestors had preserved through the dignity of labor.

Segun soon became fully conscious of his father's stand on school work, friendship, women, leisure, God and social life generally. He began to feel stifled as his expressions, needs and exuberance became too measured and lackluster. For a young man with youthful energy and outgoing by nature, such choking rules and lifestyle made him increasingly feel odd in comparison with his peers.

One major rule of Wole was that his children must speak Standard English of the most impeccable nature. Hence, within the first month of their arrival, he had rid his older children of Pidgin and Nigerian English before they got jobs and moved out. Being the only one left at home to live by such rules, Segun regarded himself as a ticking time bomb that would eventually explode once the doors of freedom were thrown open but he masked his social tendencies and tried to play by his father's rules, in his father's house.

"Daddy, there is a planned sleepover by Luther from the youth court in church. It is his birthday and he invited everyone over to their house…"

"Is that the only son of Mr. Douglas?" asked Wole.

"Yes, Daddy."

"And are his parents aware of this overnight jamboree at their residence?"

"They must be, Dad. He cannot possibly invite us all without taking permission from his parents, right?" Segun said more, rhetorically, than quizzical.

"Wake up, son, this is America," Wole said. "That boy, though not the naughty type, is an over-pampered only child. For all you know, he may have decided to try new things this time" Wole said, his suspicion growing.

"But you told me he was one of the good boys in church and I should try getting closer to such good-natured members of the youth court" Segun said, holding his Dad to his own words.

"And that hasn't changed, neither do I rule out the possibility that this our good boy may be eager to try new things. What if his parents planned to travel during this period?" Wole asked.

"I don't think so. At least, not on the birthday of their only son and besides he wouldn't have come to the church to openly share invitation cards. Besides I don't think…"

"That's enough, you have a good point. But can you forget about this invite till I run a check with his parents and let you know if you can go?" Wole said, more to silence Segun than for any other reason.

"Okay, Dad. I will go only if you approve" Segun said, knowing that an approval might never come.

"I wonder why he couldn't plan to simply celebrate his birthday at the church during your youths' court meetings. Why this elaborate residential inconvenience?" Wole wondered.

"Dad, he has friends in school, at home and other places besides the church, remember?" Segun said, silencing his father who waved his agreement and kept quiet.

Of course, the approval never came and surprisingly, the party proved to be a successful one. No record of violence and no alcohol or anything that might have triggered delinquent outbursts.

Segun fought hard to subdue his displeasure with his father.

****

Upon admission into the university, soccer became Segun's escape. He played his heart out and was very good at his game. Indeed, his prowess in the field of play was too astounding to go unnoticed. And soon he got recruited into the school's soccer team.

Segun got immersed in doing what he knew how to do best, which was exceling and making his highly expectant parents proud. He was good at soccer and soccer was also good to him, along with the pay. Sadly, he soon got consumed by the demands of soccer that he fell short in the area of academics. He was paid to play soccer by the school, while his parents expected him to be exceptional in his academics. Yet, a greater percentage of his effort tilted towards soccer.

This imbalance in joggling his passion for soccer and his academics actually made both to suffer at varying degrees as he was unable to give adequate attention to any of them. His academics suffered the more as his grades dropped. Still, he eventually managed to finish community college, and got a job.

Every young man craves for success but when failure or near-success experiences hit a young heart, the tendency is to find an escape. Segun, being well-trained, neither dabbled into drugs or women. Even the few times when party and sleepover invitations came his way, his parents never allowed that and were quite over protective about where their son went and who he spent time with. But with Segun's growing age and new full-time job came freedom—freedom to navigate his life on his terms; freedom to socialize with anybody he wished to and go wherever he so felt like.

Such unbridled freedom felt good and although he had arrived too late to the scene, he was willing to make up for lost times and so his new apartment became a beehive of activities and movements. Though he worked two jobs, one as a bank teller at the Bank of America and the other as a security guard, he still had some time on his hands to revive his social life. Segun made enough money to buy a car and this made life easier for him as he would drive from his job at the Bank of America to his security job in a hurry. He would practically battle with time and beat time to it by getting to work early. His car became not only a means of mobility for him, but also a changing room, as while driving to work, he would multi-task by wearing his uniform for his security job. This he did frantically while driving, being careful to look around and avoid bumping into anyone or anything while at it.

This became a daily routine that he pulled off so well and he was quite dedicated to his jobs. Segun was determined, in spite of his adventurous and extroverted nature, to make something out of himself that his future would be thankful for. He worked diligently, and soon discovered that aspect of him which was passionate and gave hundred percent to whatever he ventured into.

****

As Segun would soon discover, the life of an immigrant in the United States was that of two extremes of wonder and the other of worries. The wonder often arose from trying to fathom how such a large society could be so beautifully constructed and ordered, with coordinated activities and laws which the teeming population seemed fully aware of. The wonder further extended to the citizens' knowledge of the consequences of breaking such laws. Indeed, immigrants from other parts of the world who came to this beautiful country, found it difficult and indeed a shock when things taken for granted in their homelands became such an issue in their new country of residence. Hence, beyond the culture shock of mannerisms, food, sartorial choices, political dispositions and the weather, was also the murky terrain of the law.

Most immigrants who were not armed with information about how their new environments worked, often fell prey to the long arms of the law. Segun was well prepared and advised by his father on how to stay out of trouble, by limiting his circle to a few responsible friends, staying more at home and focusing on his studies. He was however not so prepared and aware of the major expectations and demands of the mainstream American society. And especially with regards to his new status as a car owner, he hardly knew what constituted a serious traffic offence beyond the general knowledge of the average car owner.

On a fateful day, Segun rounded off his last hour on his day job at Bank of America and started his routine frantic battle to beat the time and get to his night job as a guard early. He used his MapQuest and drove into the express. R. Kelly's *Hero* boomed from the stereo and serenaded him as he kept one hand busy on the steering while the other alternated between the gear and the polythene bag containing his uniform on the other car seat. His eyes also engaged in the dual task of looking in the direction of the moving vehicle and the direction of the gear and the polythene bag.

Segun suddenly realized that he was driving against his exit and became confused, his mind working almost at the speed of light, controlling his hands as the right hands worked on the gear and the other pulled out his uniform before quickly changing gear. He spotted the right exit and sped into it. And from the far left lane, he had crossed four lanes and exited after which he sped off, before gradually reducing his speed in order to wear his uniform.

Segun, in his state of rush, was oblivious of the fact that he was being followed by a police officer, who had driven ahead of him, parked her motorbike and stepped in the middle of the road to stop him. He was too distracted, working on the buttons of his shirt as he pulled them off and wore his work shirt. He fiddled with the buttons but not without briefly looking at the road in an effort to steady his hands on the steering wheel. It was on looking ahead that he discovered that a police officer had rounded off the corner, pointing her gun at his vehicle in the belief that he wanted to run her over.

He brought the car to an abrupt halt, as the officer pulled him over to the corner, reality dawning on him. His heart pounded and throbbed in his chest as his breathing heaved up and down. With shaky hands, he did last minute arrangement of the items flung around the front seat of the car, while the officer walked to his side of the car.

Coming from a country like Nigeria, Segun knew that commuters and private car owners had a singular reaction to such scenarios; in fact, it was almost like they were all indoctrinated into that singular reaction to being pulled over by policemen on any highway. They usually had some naira notes specially dedicated to policemen and also for touts in the case of commercial drivers. On such occasions, the driver would methodically bring out his hand and squeeze the money into the officer's hand and he would dramatically be waved to move on. It was called "Roger".

Segun naturally concluded that this was just a storm in a teacup as the officer would eventually ask for Roger and all would be well. The officer regarded him from the window and motioned for him to wind down the glass. But Segun in readiness to quickly settle her and get back to business as usual, opened the car door to do what he felt was the only solution.

"Get back into the car right now!" the officer commanded, rifle in hand and with a stern look that signaled danger. Segun did as he was told, now fully aware of the seriousness of the situation. Contrary to his earlier relaxed approach, he became agitated.

"Sorry, ma" he said, visibly gripped by fear and silently pleading with his eyes. It dawned on him that he was neither in Oshodi nor Ojuelegba. This was the United States of America!

"Any particular reason why you were speeding?" the officer asked, searching his face with her eyes, meeting his gaze with measured sternness, intimidating and overpowering him without the least effort.

"I have an emergency at my job; and as a security officer, I have to be there to take statements" he said.

"Why didn't they call 911, so that the police can handle the emergency?" she asked.

"I really wouldn't know if they did or not, till I get there", he replied.

The cop walked to her bike and started scribbling something on paper with her pen. She approached Segun and gave it to him.

"Ah! What is this?" Segun asked, wide-eyed.

"These are two tickets, one for seat belt and the other for speeding."

Segun quickly remembered his rich Yoruba culture, one that melted the hearts of most women; a culture in which an offended woman softened once called "Aunty", while the offender bowed or prostrated.

"Aunty, please..." he said, prostrating on the floor and searching the officer's face for any hint of approval or acceptance.

"Who is your aunty?" the officer asked, not hiding her irritation.

Segun again remembered that in Nigeria, when a woman who ought to be referred to as "Mummy", was addressed as "aunty", she was likely to get angry and consider it rude. So he tried another appeasing title, in hope that the officer would temper justice with mercy.

"Mummy, please…" he pleaded.

The officer, a Caucasian woman, became even more irritated as she looked around. "Who is your mummy? Sign the tickets!"? She commanded, her voice a little higher than normal.

Segun signed the tickets and wept all the way to work. That very day taught him a lesson and he vowed to be more informed about his environment. Upon enquiries, he learned about the common mistakes made by immigrants, one of which was DWI (Drinking While Intoxicated). He also learned that immigrants were often involved in cases of domestic violence, especially between husbands and wives, friends and even siblings. And there were also those who engaged in fighting. On further reading and research, he realized the need for anger management as most of those who fell prey equally had anger issues. This made him vow to be more circumspect as his life happened to be at two extremes, the very reason why he hadn't really achieved so much, owing to his inability to achieve balance.

When Segun was happy, he was extremely happy, and could be the life of the party, partying hard and in high spirit. When he was angry, he was extremely angry and could destroy things in a fit of anger. That singular experience with the police officer opened his eyes and taught him to be overtly aware of his society, and not take things for granted. This he buried in the recesses of his heart, and this would later change his life for good in years to come.

****

Segun's resolve to be more cautious did not last for long though. Once he finally gained admission to college, he became even more aware of his freedom and the many excesses it afforded him. He made lots of friends and was what anybody would refer to as the life of the party. He partied hard, rocking life like there was no tomorrow. He would go crazy and dance all night, never missing a chance to expend his youthful energy at either attending, organizing or hosting parties. And with no mother or father to censor his actions, "infringe on his rights", dictate or hinder his movements, he dissipated his growing and crazy passion for parties even more recklessly.

Segun abused and misused his newfound freedom to the point where he would jump from one club to the other, from Tuesday to Sunday, and have only Monday to do anything meaningful with his life. Life began to drag at snail speed, while Segun continued to catch up on all the years of deprivation from his parents, years of not allowing him to experience or take a bite of the life he now had, to the point of him wanting to do all and inadvertently overdoing everything. He had what he considered his own entertainment company, which was basically a group of youngsters, organizing and throwing all kinds of parties, but especially college parties.

Segun was indeed at a crossroads, a point in time in his life, where he wanted it all and could do all within his powers to have it all. He juggled so much all at once and his life began to gradually veer off from the direction it ought to take, and he was helpless as to how to put things in check.

It didn't take long for news about his lifestyle to travel and people began to write him off. There were stereotypes and projections made by people on the possible direction that his life was headed and where he was likely to end up. He became increasingly aware of the fact that people around didn't hold him in high esteem and would openly conclude, often to his hearing, that he was a candidate for jail.

Segun soon noticed the change in the disposition of church members towards him. Parents would keep their children from engaging in friendly chats with him after service, saying that he had gotten nothing to offer them.

One day, after church, Segun sighted Luther standing near the exit. "Hey Luther, been a while, where and how have you been?" Segun asked his buddy.

"Travelled two states away for my housemanship. Just came home to spend a little time with my parents before travelling back to my base" replied Luther.

"Dr. Luther! That is great and I am proud of you and I know your parents will be so happy about your giant strides. Look at you mehn, my brother. Keep it up and keep making your parents and the rest of us proud.

Let's catch a drink or see a move after church next Sunday. I will call to…"

"Luther!" came his mother's stern voice from the entrance of the church where she had spotted her son with Segun.

"A minute, Mum, I am talking with a friend", Luther replied.

"Come right now, Luther," his mother insisted.

"Wait a minute, Segun, I will be right back," Luther said, hurrying to his mother.

"What's wrong, Mum? You look like you've just seen a ghost!" Luther, said, regarding his mum with the searching eyes of a doctor.

"A ghost would have been better. Stay away from that young man. He is no good for you. He is a bad influence and may get you in trouble."

"Mum, I am not a child, I am not easily influenced and I respect people's need to be themselves and enjoy themselves…"

"Stop it, Luther. I said he is nothing but trouble. I don't want you to get into trouble, you have a great life ahead of you. Be selective about who you hang out with," Mrs. Douglas retorted.

"Okay, let me at least say goodbye to him, he is waiting for me…" pleaded Luther as he turned to reach for Segun, but saw him quickly walking away, first increasing his pace before running off.

"Mum I think he heard everything you said?" Luther said, concern and worry etched on his face. Mrs. Douglas propelled her son to the car while quickly changing the subject of their discussion.

Segun ran home, feeling angry but eventually shrugged it off. How many times had he heard such unsavory statements? He held unto his vow to prove his critics wrong. He would show them that being social did not in any way amount to being irresponsible, and that even partying was a modern way of relieving stress.

Though people's comments and looks hurt him and brought about a deep-seated feeling of inadequacy to Segun, he was however helpless in redeeming himself or even earning a tiny corner in their good books. In fact, he was done trying to do so. He was only grateful that time had helped him to develop a thick skin to look beyond their comments to the glorious future he was sure awaited him.

Unsurprisingly, for the second time, history repeated itself in Segun's academic life as his school works and grades suffered due to his inability to achieve a balance between his school work and social life. This was the exact same challenge he faced at Community College, as he couldn't achieve equilibrium between his academics and his career in football. It became quite a daunting task, doing justice to his school work and things slowed down.

Segun's new apartment which was not so close to his parents', was his priceless gift and he welcomed friends and friends of friends. He visited his parents often, though, and also met up with them in church on Sundays.

The dedication of the Bankoles to the church was a deep-rooted one, since it was there that Segun's father had found solace as a new immigrant in America. He had lived a little with the pastor before getting his own apartment. And the administrative job he got at the church helped a lot before getting a second job and then getting an entirely promising career outside of the church. He however remained a dedicated member and worker in the church and carried his family along in this direction. This meant that his family were familiar to members of the church and news about their activities had a way of being known by church members in such a close-knit community.

On one Sunday, Segun had dressed his best and looked good as he would be meeting up with his parents and possibly follow them home for lunch. It was a cold Sunday morning and Segun had driven to the church early. He got the stares that he was now so accustomed to, stares that held so many unanswered questions, stares ridden with prejudice and unspoken assumptions.

As always, he walked into the church, defying people's judgement of him. Gospel music wafted in the air and Segun always felt mortified by the ambience of the church, that atmosphere that brought tranquility and caused him to reflect. And irrespective of the way he was profiled by some members, the church would always be home for him.

The choir made service a delight as they sang their hearts out and literally brought down the heavens. Some people in the neighborhood attended service just to get lifted by the heavenly voices of the singers and sometimes, notable gospel artistes who were either members of the church or special guests who, during special occasions, graced the service with their unique talents.

In spite of the unstable nature of Segun's social life, he was a church boy through and through. From Nigeria, and back to the United States, Segun had a pulling force that was lodged deep in his Christian background, which often pulled him back to the ancient path even when he seemed to have gone astray. There seemed to

70

be a seventh hand that validated years of intercession made over his life and future by his parents and spiritual leaders who were close to the family and often conducted prayers upon his parents' request. Hence while living the groovy life, he still loved God and had a soft spot for Him. This is the reason why the negative vibes he receives from his fellow brethren sometimes had a deep emotional effect on him.

"It is testimony time, brethren, and we believe that the Lord has dealt marvelously with some of us in the past days and it will be great to share his goodness with the Church so we can tap into such testimonies," resonated the preacher's voice from the pulpit.

A couple of members shared their testimonies, but one stood out. That was the testimony by a Ghanaian, Edward Asante, who had just moved to the States. Edward's voice was laden with so much excitement.

"Praise the Lord with me, brethren, for he has again seen my plight and located me in this foreign land by sending his angels to pay my bills. I don't know how he did it, but it has been an awesome and amazing journey since my three months of sojourn in this land," he said as the church chorused "Hallelujah" in unison and he proceeded with his testimony.

"I went to Macy's fashion mall and purchased some stuffs. One of the sales personnel introduced me to the process of opening a credit in order to get 20% off items. I signed and they gave me credit card. When I made my way to the payment section to pay for the very items they had just sold to me, I was told that my bills had already been cleared, courtesy of the credit card I applied for. I don't know how these things work but such freebies made me realize the seriousness of God's divine providence and …." His voice trailed off as the congregation burst into roaring laughter.

It was obvious to everyone that Edward did not understand how credit card worked and the fact that he was digitally charged for all the items he purchased. The pastor started explaining the process to him as Segun stood up to ease himself at the gents. The pastor's voice halted him midway along the church aisle

"Segun! We are here trying to correct a brother, and instead of you to sit and learn, you are walking out of the church. Do you think you are better than him or incapable of making the same mistake? This is why your life is this way. My son, you need humility and you also need to walk constantly in the way of the Lord. Anyway, back to you, Brother Edward Asante…" the pastor went on and on, about credit cards and how they worked in a cashless economy. And it dawned on Brother Edward that far from the cash economy of Ghana, he was now operating in a cashless economy and must upgrade his knowledge of how things worked.

Segun on the other hand felt the jab of the preacher's words and lowered his head in a failed attempt to control his anger. He finished his business at the gents and went back to his seat. His mind got totally distracted from the voice on the pulpit, even while his head was a turmoil of multiple voices, uttering statements that he had heard in the past, from people who ought to show him love, but who rather judged him mercilessly.

Yes, he had made some bad decisions and had overindulged his social cravings but a little faith could have gone a long way. He closed his eyes to shut out the voices in his head but those adamant voices came in violent flood and he yielded and waited for them to pronounce their negative verdicts thus:

"I don't want my children hanging around someone like that... Look at your mates, they are making it and you are here gallivanting... That one is going to end up in jail... What kind of a mother will have or raise a child like that... He cannot possibly amount to anything at the rate he is going."

These voices came in quick succession, haunting him and causing a chaotic storm in his subconscious. He buried his face in his hands to ward them off but they defied his fights till they outlived their span and trailed off, leaving him an emotional mess. He had indeed been stripped of his dignity and it was now on him to prove them wrong. They had profiled him, branded him a prodigal, an incurable recalcitrant but the joke would be on them because he would set the record straight.

The service was dismissed amidst shouts of "Hosanna in the highest" and Segun headed for the exit, without looking back, without exchanging pleasantries. He totally forgot his lunch plans at his parents'. His anger had brimmed and he needed to cool off. His bed at home called on him and his pillows would be the right shoulders to weep on. He fastened his shaky and sweaty hands around the steering and sped off, leaving a fog of dust in his trail as he ran to the sanctuary of his home to preserve his sanity, a sanctuary full of his kind - roommates and squatters who would never judge or profile him.

Five
PRICE OF LIBERTY

With the church no longer welcoming, Segun drew closer to his peers for solace. He became the toast of his pals and his house became the abode of restless, strayed and helpless souls. He was generous to a fault and his companions took advantage of it. Tunde, Kofi, Tochi, Sly, Dumelo and George amongst others were the people who frequently visited his apartment till they all forgot where they came from and became more like roommates and squatters in Segun's home.

The distraction and inconvenience were to a choking level but Segun would rather have that than an empty apartment, barren of liveliness and fraught with cemetery silence. Their arguments, banters, games and the interactive nights of football watching and betting, and game nights, were things to look forward to.

"My father has a mansion in Accra but I am squatter in the United States. Can you beat that?" lamented Kofi as he laughed hysterically, masking his disappointment in a masculine demeanor that said he didn't care but the truth is, he was at a breaking point.

"I sold my shop at Kumasi for his trip but I am yet to even get a job as an ordinary sales assistant in my new country. How about that?" Dumelo sighed.

"Guys, you all chose the lives you now live; so I suggest we stop lamenting and focus on how to make the best of it" George advised.

"We weren't properly advised, that's for sure. And starting school afresh was a big mistake for people of our age. The best option would have been to evaluate our certificates and pursue higher degrees, instead of starting undergraduate studies afresh. I just wish I could turn back the hands of time, I would have proceeded to the Masters level with my Engineering Studies at Obafemi Awolowo University," Tunde regretted.

"Hey guys, I have had a rough day," Segun interjected. "I think we should change the subject and just breathe. This place is too cramped for negative energy and vibes, we will just choke here. I have ice cream and pizza."

"I will survive either by hook or crook," Sly vowed, not ready to give up the discussion yet. "I didn't cross the Atlantic to come and count bridges over here. I mean, I made it down here with my own blood; so I either make it or die trying to do so. I ain't going back to Sierra Leone a pauper. How many are we here? We can form a gang of survivors and take whatever this land has to offer, either willingly or forcefully. It has got to yield to our increase."

Sly eyed the rest of the crew and silently cursed them for being so downright sanctimonious.

Segun stared at Sly for a while. There was always something dark about him. In fact, his presence in the house often unsettled Segun who constantly corrected and tried to put him in check. He once drove out with Segun's car and bashed a parked vehicle while over-speeding and he ran all the way home without stopping to apologise or check the extent of damage. Segun had already hinted it to Tunde that he would oust him from his apartment to avoid his negative vibes and incessant animosity. They were still looking for a way to do so without coming across as doing so. It was complicated but Sly was a handful.

"Sly, what about me?" Segun asked, somewhat angry. "I left my university education in Nigeria. I graduated from a community college with a poor grade, due to my inability to strike a balance between extracurricular and academics. But here I am, giving my degree another shot and still making the exact same mistake.

But I would rather try again and again that give up or commit crime. I brought you in because I felt that if I could help you to temporarily solve the challenge of accommodation, you would take life by the lapels and do justice to your stay in this country but I guess I was expecting too much because you incite violence and recklessness and this house, including all of us have become too small for you. You were one hell of a godly chap when you turned up at my doorstep with our mutual friend, Rosy. What happened to you, man?"

"There is a devil even in godly people, Segun. America pissed on my goodwill and I must now take my survival in my hands," said Sly, forming a fist.

"Then not in my house, Sly. If you must sell your soul to the devil, my home will not be your auction yard or bargaining table. I tried, Bro, your time's up," Segun declared.

"You have tried for me, for all of us, Segun but I am sorry, I do not share your ideologies. We are too different to cohabit and I figured this out a long time and have been looking for a place. Don't worry about me, guys. I will be fine as I already have somewhere to go. Thanks, Bro, I appreciate" Sly said, smiling warily.

Sly extended his hands in a handshake and both men shook hands and managed a hug before parting ways. A calm descended in the apartment and the rest of the guys voiced their misgivings about him before carrying on with their initial banter about life in America.

****

Segun's visitors would sometimes cross their boundaries and wear his clothes, shoes and accessories. Sometimes they used his laptops and had their choice programs running on TV for hours without end in which case Segun would just watch their programs without changing the station as the remote was hardly ever in his hands. But they respected him and kept to the few boundaries he had given them upon bringing them into his home. They often drove in his car to wherever they wished to go to and whenever they deemed fit. Segun was their hero and favorite guy and he basked in the euphoria of being a low-key boss man.

Nigerians would often say that the locusts that would invade a nation usually came in ones and twos. The youngsters came in ones and twos, and gradually became an inevitable part of Segun's life, a part that he could not divorce himself from. At a time, his spirit was a bit troubled for days but he couldn't lay his hand on the cause of his soul's restlessness. He wondered if he had overdone himself this time as he noticed that some of the young men were downright irresponsible and reckless. But he shrugged it off as some of the things that young people often did, silently assuring himself that they would outgrow their excesses.

79

Segun soon discovered what he felt would be the perfect solution to the unceasing restlessness of soul that he had been experiencing. He decided to attend the convention of a popular church nearby. He booked a hotel a bit far from the venue, as he needed an alone time while at it. This was more like a retreat from everything that threatened to make him cave in to anger and depression. And the church's convention promised him the revival that he craved.

After the convention, he drove north in the direction of his hotel but soon got pulled over by a police officer.

"Young man, do you know why I pulled you over? She asked, searching his face.

"No." he replied, more confused than ever.

"Well, you were speeding. Can I have your license?" She demanded, as Segun went back to his vehicle and fetched his license and handed it over to her.

"Can you verify your name for me, one more time"? She requested, a frown forming around her lips.

"My name is Segun Bankole" he replied

"You know, I have to place you under arrest, right? She asked, quite certain that he was aware of his crime.

"Why would you do that? You are only pulling me over for speeding, just write me a ticket. Since when did you people start arresting people for speeding?" he asked, a trifle impatiently.

She regarded him once more, a bit confused at his reaction but ignored him nonetheless and said, "I have a warrant for your arrest."

"What?!"

"I have a warrant for the arrest of the owner of this vehicle, the person who bears this name," the officer said, pointing at his name tag on his driver's license. "Is this your name?" she asked again.

"Yes, this is my name but I can never be the man that you are looking for. I mean, what would be my crime?" he replied, shrugging off the fear rearing its ugly head up inside of him.

"The crime is credit card fraud. And going by the name I have here, which you have affirmed to be yours, you are the man I am looking for." she said, opening the door for him to step out.

Everything happened in split seconds and played out before Segun's eyes like one forcefully led to the cinema to watch his own horror movie with an empty bowl of unpopped popcorn forced into his hands. He gnashed his teeth in pain as the officer locked the handcuffs around his wrists amidst protests.

"I am not the man you are looking for, he said, as she pushed him gently into the backseat of her patrol van. Her male partner came around and started the car. Segun realized that this was neither a prank or a joke and began to weep. He remembered all that people had said about his life and future and silently asked God if this was how his life would end, if he would allow the world to make a mockery of His glory over his life. He realized he was in deep trouble and began praying violently and incoherently in tongues, calling "Jesus" at intervals to have mercy on him and save his soul from damnation. The officer who could no longer hide his pity finally spoke up during the ride.

"You know, some of the great men in the Bible were tried and prosecuted for crimes they did not commit but they came out triumphant and vindicated. Something in me tells me that you are not the man we are looking for," the officer said.

And at that moment, Segun connected with his faith and realized that it was God speaking to him. The officer continued:

"I have seen things, especially misfortune turn around to fortune and glory in my line of career. I know when I have arrested a criminal and when I have the wrong person placed under arrest. It comes with years of experience," she said and turned around to face the window while Segun broke into a song, sobbing along while at it, silently wondering the drama that would play out at the station. He thought of all the people that had written him off as a candidate for prison and wondered why he ended up here just when he was making an effort to prove them wrong. He really didn't want this to happen and have led a clean life but somehow he was in this police vehicle in handcuffs, and under arrest for a crime he had never imagined, let alone carried out.

Segun was taken to a holding cell, where his information was taken down and a few pictures taken for records purposes. He could not sleep and stayed awake all night. They gave him food and drink but he turned them down, praying and crying all through. It was the most humiliating night of his life. He was soon led to the interrogation room where he stayed alone for a while, as the prosecutor and the interrogator spoke behind the glass, scribbling things down before making their way to the two seats in front of him. They exchanged greetings with him before bombarding him with questions that he was obliged to answer in order to bring closure to what really happened and who was responsible.

"What is your name?" they inquired

"I am Segun Bankole," he said as he watched them

exchange quick glances. They asked a dozen other questions.

"Do you know why and how we got your information?" the female officer asked

"I have no idea," he replied. She brought out a picture of a car and asked, "Is this your vehicle?"

"Yes, this is my car," Segun replied, still confused.

"If this is your vehicle, we were able to retrieve a footage of your vehicle, after you committed the crime. Here are the pictures of you, committing the crime. And in fact, we went back to take footage of you at the moment you carried out the crime" they said, placing pictures on the table for him to remember and start talking.

But Segun was totally lost, staring at the pictures, turning them over to identify which of the occupants in his small apartment could have done this while out with his car. If anything was certain, he was not the man in the picture and it was evident. But with the face of the fellow a bit blurred, Segun could not find other pointers to direct the attention of the officers to, in order to prove his innocence.

"Officer, I am not the man in the picture! I don't wear wrist watches. I have never owned or worn one because I am allergic. I am not as tall as the man in the picture.

We may be of the same build but we are definitely not the same people. Besides he has an afro and a darker skin shade than I," Segun said, but the officers didn't seem convinced as all other evidence pointed in his direction.

Segun gave his proof of innocence another shot and went on defending himself,

"Officer, agreed, this is my car, but this is not me. In fact, I think I know the fellow in this picture but I cannot say exactly where he is."

"You know what? I believe you" the female officer finally said, looking him in the eye. "But if you are saying that this is not you, then you must also be willing to identify who he is and where we can find him," she said.

"I can make a good guess of who this fellow is, but I cannot say exactly where he is. As at the date of this crime as stated by you, he was still living in my house, but I have since asked him to leave my house and so I can't say exactly where he is at the moment" Segun said, eyes beseeching the officers.

"I believe you but I cannot help you. Since we cannot find the person in these pictures and video and all the evidence available points to you," the officer said with measured difficulty.

The United States is a country whose legal system thrives on evidence and hard facts. Since the crime was committed using Segun's car, it was enough to proceed with the case. He was charged and had his day in court. He realized at that moment that one mistake an immigrant must never make in America was to get into problems with the law and get arrested for a crime. He learned that even if a person arrested for a crime was not guilty of the crime, it would still be in the record that he or she was arrested for such, and it would be there for a long time.

It took a while before Segun could find a lawyer that could represent him. His lawyer tried to find out the person in the picture and they eventually made headway with their search. On meeting Sly face to face, he immediately knew that something was wrong, as he spoke as though he had prepared for such a day as this.

"I figure you already suspect why we are here," Segun said to his former friend. "You have to come forward and tell the court that it was you and not me, so the court can drop the case against me. I really need to move forward with my life and this is putting me in a bad place," said Segun pleadingly.

"Unfortunately, I cannot do this at the moment. I am currently working on my citizenship. If you can bear this for a while, let me file for citizenship, get citizenship and then come forward", Sly said, in the most selfish and annoying manner.

"But you committed this crime, Bro! I am not the guilty one here, so why make me pay for what you did? If you knew you would be filing for citizenship, then why did you go committing credit card fraud?" he shot back at him.

"See I can imagine your predicament," Sly said. "Just give me a little time, I will take responsibility for my actions but if I come forward right now, they will definitely deport me, Segun!" he said with a tone of finality.

Segun sank to the floor in exhaustion and anger at the extent of betrayal and the calculated nature of this fellow who had committed this crime with his car within visible distance, as though he had deliberately meant to set him up. He realized he was in conversation with a cold-hearted human and hence, flogging a dead horse.

Sly eventually got his citizenship, but instead of owning up to his crime, he suggested that Segun accept the deal offered by the prosecutor, after which he, Sly, would give 10,000 dollars to him for all the troubles. Segun walked out on him and went to seek the face of God. He prayed endlessly, fasted and sang in tongues. He beseeched the heavens to come to his rescue and not allow the world to laugh at him.

Something unbelievable happened after that. The prosecutor went to the judge and told him that he believed Segun's story. He asked the judge to withdraw the case while they looked for the fellow who committed the crime.

Segun received this news with a sigh of relief. Still, he knew that he would have many hurdles to cross, as the stain would remain in his record for a long time. He had even come to terms that his life might be on hold and he would probably not get a job or that he might just get something that was way below his qualifications, owing to the presence of such history of crime and arrest in his record. But he was happy that a great battle was won and he could go home and rebuild his life. He vowed to make a new fire from the ashes of this ordeal.

Segun made up his mind to work till his dreams became a reality. He became so resolute that he began a thorough sanitation of his apartment, a move that only symbolized starting afresh. He painted his walls, changed the blinds, discarded all junks, dismissed all those hanging around his home, had a long shower and slept for a very long time. He woke up, shopped for new groceries from the apartment store opposite his street. He got home, cleaned out his fridge and stocked it with new fresh items. He made a good meal and relished the experience of having a home-made meal after such a long time.

Segun tuned in to his favorite TV station while eating the popcorn he had popped in the microwave. He knew deep down that he would never be the same again, that something in him had changed and that there would be no place in his life for failure or mediocrity. He picked up his Bible and the page that opened up to him was Isaiah 28:16 "This, now, is what the Sovereign Lord says: 'I am placing in Zion a foundation that is firm and strong. In it I am putting a solid cornerstone on which are written the words, *Faith that is firm is also patient*". He meditated on this till he slept off, firmly clutching the Bible to his chest.

Six
BACK TO THE ANCIENT PATH

It is a common saying that America never forgets. Old and aged octogenarian Americans may come down with senility or Alzheimer's disease but America thrives on archiving and record-keeping, a culture that ensures that even after a crime is prosecuted and an offender serves the stipulated jail term, the history of arrest and crime remains on cyberspace for all to see. This is a highly accessible data that can only be erased after an agreed number of years and also depending on the enormity of the crime committed.

Although Segun had been discharged and acquitted, his past followed him along the streets of the United States like a shadow, almost like a second skin that he could never shrug off or pretend like it never happened. He applied for jobs endlessly but without success. His record remained tainted by the stain of another man's crime, the ultimate price of his lack of caution and his uncensored generosity. He withdrew into his shells, afraid to make friends because he had come to terms with his weakness, the fact that he could never be sure again how far he could go to keep the people in his life happy and comfortable to his own detriment.

For some time, he went solo, a loner, moving from company to company, applying to each and every job that had any connection to his expertise or experience, but coming back each time, a wounded lion. His pride was blotted by that singular experience. Sometimes he would get to the interview stage before he was once again directed to the exit. It became a stigma he would have to live with, at least, till it was finally expunged from his record.

One day, however, fortune seemed to have smiled on Segun. He applied for a job, using someone else's name and information. He finally got the job and was sitting in a boardroom where the new employees had convened for the orientation. This was a job that promised to pay him twelve dollars per hour and that was a good start for a man who had searched endlessly for a job. Though the guilt of impersonation put him in great discomfort, the fact was that his circumstances had made him so vulnerable.

During the orientation, the management played a certain video to motivate the workforce and spur them on to stellar service delivery. This, however, became the kick that Segun's conscience had yearned for, a turning point in his life. He suddenly got up, packed up his stuff and walked out of the building.

"Where are you going? We are not done for the day" called out one of the managers to Segun, as he walked towards the exit.

"Don't worry, you can keep your job now," he said, waving his hands up as though in total surrender.

The video was about a man called Eric Thomas, popularly addressed as the hip-hop preacher, whose story seemed almost similar to that of Segun. He had been a homeless man with neither a degree nor a high school diploma, a dropout who had lived in abandoned buildings, picking trash and surviving without a roadmap. He had however struggled against all odds to become a force to be reckoned with. Eric, from nothing and out of nowhere, with neither the support of kin nor society, made something out of his life.

In the video, Eric said "the moment you want to succeed as bad as you want to breathe, that is when you start being successful. For those who have been immersed in water for baptism, they will understand that fleeting seconds of breathlessness. And for those who have survived drowning, who know what it means to grab onto a last straw, they will be home with this quote and the imagery it evokes. When you fight for your breath, you would naturally fight, kick, scratch, splash and keep your head afloat and above water just to keep from losing your breath. If this is how bad you want to succeed in life, then you will surely be great in life."

Segun knew he had a history of dropping out of school and not finishing well at one point due to his history of lack of balance between two competing ends in his life. This singular record made him realize the crucial role he must play when he became a father, which was helping his children to achieve a relative certainty as to what they wanted to do with their lives and the career path that they were inclined to, and thus help them to achieve it. And this must be done early in order that history would not repeat itself as this would help to forestall incidents of dropping out from university or being caught between two careers with no idea of which one should have the upper hand.

Segun walked out of that building, a totally transformed man. He went home, laid flat on his back and stared at his white ceiling. He reflected on his life, his successes and high points, his pitfalls and low points. He vowed never to deprive his children of their freedom but to love, support and trust them. He would protect them while acknowledging first their ability to protect themselves. He would equip them with digital knowledge and gadgets, while teaching them the discipline on the usage of those things in order to nip addiction in the bud. He would never compare them to outsiders or to each other in other not to bruise their confidence and self-esteem. He would listen to them in order to be their trusted pal, as this would prevent them from seeking validation from outsiders and falling prey to multiple conflicting voices and peer pressure. He came to terms with the weaknesses of his upbringing and came to the point where he must take decisive action to bring his life back on track. He had started out with Accounting and failed at it, and majored in Business Management and later Computer Science. That night, Segun decisively made up his mind to start a degree in Information Systems Project Management. He prayed fervently for the heavens to bless his new line of interest and help him to do justice to this one and finish strong.

****

Segun, now ready for his degree to take off, remained a bachelor but ready for a serious relationship, as he wasn't getting any younger. He didn't want to rush into any commitments for fear of falling into the wrong hands. Life had dished him his fair share of ups and downs and he now deliberately threaded with caution.

In the meantime, Segun managed a gospel artiste while

searching for his dream job. Segun and Dami Jacobs, the gospel artiste he managed, would honor invitations to gospel concerts and in the process, network and get referrals for their next show. He did this on the side while searching for the job of his dreams.

On a particular Sunday, after a concert, Segun met a certain lady who introduced herself as Rebecca, and that became the beginning of new things in his life. He would call her up and they would encourage each other, their joys and pains while projecting for a future that they both dreamed off. Though Segun didn't know much about falling in love, he was sure that Rebecca, who he loved to call Ruby, held him in high regard and that seemed enough for him.

"You are the first person the call me up today. So, how have you been Ruby?" Segun asked, during one of their phone chats.

"I am fine, Segs, just bored and want to step out for the movies, do you mind? Rebecca asked.

"If we are not going Dutch, then I mind, I am so low on cash, Ruby" he managed to say.

"Hey boo, relax, I got this. I will pay for both of us, dear. Leave that to me," Rebecca said.

"You know, I really don't deserve you, Ruby," Segun said in an emotion laden voice. "You should go for someone else. You deserve a man that can take care of you more than I ever can. I have nothing Rebecca."

This dampened her excitement as she managed to say it the best way she could.

"That hurts, Segun. I already know all that but beyond your present financial status, you still hold great prospects. And no man can possibly give me more than you do. It is beyond cash and fun, dear. But you need time to convince yourself that you really want this. I will just go grab a cup of ice-cream and cool off. Later, dear."

She said and hung up. Segun bit his tongue and cursed for always saying the wrong things to Rebecca, for not knowing the best way or the right way to express his well-meaning feelings towards her.

He had relocated to San Antonio for school, with only forty dollars to his name. He purposely avoided Nigerian churches, to avoid mingling and getting distracted from his goals. Segun was a flamboyant guy and like bees to honey, he attracted people to himself. He made friends easily and that was both his strength and weakness. He however ended up in a church where he met Pastor Kola, who counseled him like a father and supported him. And through him, he got a job as a church administrator, which helped him to help out around the church, and also enabled him to make extra money to his name.

About the same period Segun settled into life in San Antonio, Rebecca came for an interview in San Antonio and got the job.

"Hello, Segs, guess what?" cooed Rebecca.

"You are visiting San Antonio?"

"Well close but not exactly. It is more than a visit. I just got a job in San Antonio and will be moving there in a few days because my appointment is immediate," she said, not hiding her excitement.

"Wow, babe, so happy for you darling. This is… this is great news" Segun said. He could beat his chest boldly and say that this wonder woman came for him. And he was done fighting the connection between them and the responsibilities that came with it. She would be in San Antonio and that held the promise of strengthening their nascent relationship and careers.

****

Though Segun was a bit laidback at the beginning, the influence of divinity on the circumstances surrounding his meeting Rebecca, their eventual relocation and relationship made him come to terms with his choice. The presence of Rebecca in his life commanded a certain level of responsibility, and ensured he was level-headed. While he schooled, Rebecca worked smart at her job and they met each other halfway.

After years of diligent effort, painstaking and calculated strides, Segun finally bagged a degree in Information Systems Project Management. And this set him on the right path towards a successful career.

It had been seven years of staying in what Segun considered his wilderness years, waiting for his arrest history to be removed from his record. It had been made clear to him by his lawyer that it would take seven years to rid his record of that history.

Shortly after his graduation, Segun married his sweetheart, Rebecca, and felt even more compelled to clean his record and start afresh on a good note. So he reached out to the prosecutor that handled his case and he was directed to the department in charge. It was in the process of all these that he realized that what took him seven years to wait for, could have taken two years to be accomplished.

Segun was told that his case would be presented before a judge for approval. He had sleepless nights, tossing and turning in bed, wondering if the judge would honor his request. But after days of anxiety, he reminded himself that the worst that could happen was that the judge would refuse to grant his request and ask him to come back after a year or two. So he braced himself up for whatever outcome that would ensue. But the judge honored his request and at last, the one thing that had haunted him for years, affected his confidence, and followed him to every organization that he went to for employment, had finally been lifted off his shoulder. A stigma and burden that had hung over his neck like an albatross, had finally been taken off. He went to a quiet corner and shed very hot tears of joy. He was uncontrollable and not even the eventual presence of Rebecca could stop the tears from streaming down. Now his life would take a different shape, he would make bolder steps and experience renewed confidence.

The saying is indeed true that once a man is diligent in his labor, the universe cooperates to favor and honor him. Segun soon got a job at one of the top five countries in the world, an IT firm. A lot of candidates had applied for that job but Segun was chosen out of the lot. Segun was so grateful for the opportunity. He held his bosses in high regard, so much that whenever he was given a task to execute, he beat the given deadline and also performed better than expected, thereby exceeding expectations.

His boss, a Spanish woman, was so impressed that when a managerial position was available, she examined his resume, pointing out the flaws that could deny him the opportunity of being promoted to the available managerial position. She practically rewrote his resume. She became his mentor, his godmother, who would go as far as advising him in all other aspects of his life, including marriage and family, whenever he solicited for advice. She became someone he could go to and unburden his mind.

"Congratulations, Segun. This is a big role with bigger responsibilities but I trust your dogged and resilient spirit" said Mrs. Sanchez.

"Thank you so much, ma, for this opportunity and for trusting me enough to prepare me for this role. God bless you" Segun said as words failed him.

"Hey, c'mon, you earned it, Segun, I did nothing but point out how you should package what you already achieved. Congrats again. I hope you're taking wifey to dinner to celebrate this feat" Mrs. Sanchez teased.

"Certainly, ma'am, if she hadn't run the home front right, I might not have been predisposed to responding effectively to office duties. So, yes, it is our victory," Segun said, trying to impress his boss who often acted as his marriage counsellor and adviser.

"I am glad you're catching on fast. Impressive! Time to get back to the pile on my desk. I owe you one," said Mrs. Sanchez as she hung up. Segun knew his time had come and he was in for a season of greatness and he seized the opportunity to groom others coming after him.

In Segun's new role, he managed a high performing team charged with controlling a very high dollar amount, hence the team made money for the company, making the company one with a net worth of over 20 billion dollars. Though the beginning was rough, as Segun was a bit overwhelmed by the expectations placed on his very young shoulder, he managed to make something wonderful out of his life, thereby proving his detractors and nay-sayers wrong! His team was a formidable one and practically gave everything to their jobs as Segun didn't fail to speak and motivate them during their strategy sessions in which they took turns to state their highs and lows and complement each other's weaknesses.

Segun deliberately started what he called the pitch session in which the team took turns bi-monthly, to pitch for better and more effective ways of achieving their yearly financial markup for the company and ensuring stellar service delivery. They also pointed out the gaps in their existing strategies and ways to bridge such gaps. Segun knew he was blessed with a good team and he stopped at nothing to ensure that they were emotionally, socially and corporately balanced as that would ensure greater productivity. He would advise, counsel and even arrange team bonding wherein they hung out and connected at a more social level.

Seven
BECOMING THE CAPSTONE

"The stone the builders rejected, has become the corner stone"

(Psalm 118:22)

Segun Bankole became a household name across the cities of America, as he went about delivering presentations and providing a solution-based service to a teeming population of people in need of mentorship, guidance or a life coach. He advised parents to loosen up a bit and reduce their default high-handedness in raising their kids and make them friends instead so they can effectively bridge the communication gap and be involved in their decision making.

He insisted that such methods would only make the children defensive, lose trust in them and shut them out of their lives eventually. And this would in turn make them to make very poor and bad decisions in life. He encouraged parents to understand the time in which their children were born, the jet age, the age of digital revolution and as millennials, they must be equipped digitally in order to compete favorably with their peers. He suggested that they buy them gadgets that they could use to navigate and enhance their knowledge of digital technology and culture.

He also held sessions in which he advised immigrants to try as much as possible to avoid doing things that would warrant them being arrested. These, he said, included fraud, anger, fighting and domestic violence. He further assured them that their African certificates were valid, as they only had to evaluate them in order to make them relevant within the American corporate space and make them tenable for employments and contracts.

Segun helped multitudes of young immigrants in preparing their resumes and making them viable for employment, just as Mrs. Sanchez had helped him. He often shared his life lessons and story, in order that others could learn from him and rise from grass to grace, from zero to hero and turn their mess into a message.

Segun conquered his mountains; his life story was indeed that of conquest. A story comparable to that of David defeating Goliath. God truly chose that which everyone had cast off, profiled and concluded to be useless and made the capstone. After his events, he would go to a corner and connect with the force that held with his might and invisible hands, propelled him to the glorious future he now lived, God. He stopped at nothing in telling people to connect with their Maker and not run faster than Him as that would only lead them to pitfalls and gridlocks. Segun patiently entertained many questions while asking strategic questions to his ever energetic crowd of listeners. He welcomed speaking invitations and one event always led to the referral for his next big outing.

Thank God that man is not God, as God wields the ultimate power and will give the last verdict. The journey to becoming a capstone is that of survival and of dreams coming through. Segun Bankole, who once was tried, charged and acquitted with a documented record of a crime he didn't commit, had become a capstone and a highly sought-after gem!

ABOUT THE AUTHOR

Omotoyosi Adebayo is a husband and father of a baby girl (Heaven). He is a graduate of the great Texas A&M university school system. He received his bachelor's degree in Information Systems and Project Management, and currently working on his Master of Business Administration degree.

Presently working at a fortune five company as a Data Analytics Manager, he has also had the pleasure and privilege of working in various industries ranging from I.T and healthcare to banking and finance and more.

An exceptional leader, with great mentoring abilities, he is passionate about using his mentoring skills to encourage young adults to unlock their potential as capstones.